# RICA BAPTISTA

## LLAMAS, IGUANAS, AND
### my VERY BEST FRIEND

# RICA BAPTISTA

## LLAMAS, IGUANAS, AND my VERY BEST FRIEND

## Janet Costa Bates

ILLUSTRATED BY Gladys Jose

CANDLEWICK PRESS

Text copyright © 2022 by Janet Costa Bates
Illustrations copyright © 2022 by Gladys Jose

First edition 2022

Library of Congress Catalog Card Number 2021953324
ISBN 978-1-5362-1630-1

22 23 24 25 26 27 LBM 10 9 8 7 6 5 4 3 2 1

Printed in Melrose Park, IL, USA

This book was typeset in ITC Giovanni.
The illustrations were created digitally.

Candlewick Press
99 Dover Street
Somerville, Massachusetts 02144

www.candlewick.com

A JUNIOR LIBRARY GUILD SELECTION

To Michael and Christian, my endless
source of inspiration
JCB

To my two very best friends,
Jessica and Vanessa
GJ

# CONTENTS

# ONE
## One Small Thing

One small thing. I was only asking for one small thing. A pet.

I didn't even care what kind. A llama. An iguana. A potbellied pig. Actually, a baby pygmy goat would probably make me the most popular kid in the entire town. Not that I wanted to be the most popular kid, since I wouldn't like being noticed that much. I just wanted to know that I could be the most popular kid—you know, if I wanted to.

The real reason I wanted a pet had nothing to do with being popular, but I couldn't tell anyone since I wasn't supposed to know.

"Any ideas for pet names yet?" asked Laini, making a free throw in my driveway without even trying. Laini Shanahan is my very best friend. Actually, she's my *only* best friend, but if I had more than one best friend, she would still be my very best.

"Maybe Frederica," I answered.

"Uh, I'm pretty sure that's your name," said Laini.

"Yeah, but everybody calls me Rica," I said. "I could say to all the world, 'I, Frederica Baptista, hereby bestow the name Frederica onto my pet pygmy goat or maybe a baby chimp—I don't know yet—but, whatever, I, myself, will hereby forth forever be known as just Rica.'"

"What did your mom say about a pet?" asked Laini.

"She said no almost faster than her mouth could open," I answered. My shot hit the backboard and bounced off.

"What about your dad?" asked Laini as she caught the basketball and passed it back to me.

"He said no as quickly as my mother did. If I'd asked them together, they would have said no in perfect harmony." I dribbled the basketball a few times and then passed it back to Laini.

"Maybe they will change their minds," said Laini as she tried to make a backward free throw. She missed, but that didn't stop her from trying again.

"Are you kidding? When I asked again—because it's always worth trying again—they wrote out a list of reasons why I shouldn't get a pet. They actually wrote it down. On paper! In pen! They can't even erase any of it!"

"What's on the list?" she asked.

I took a folded-up piece of paper out of my pocket. We sat on the porch steps as I read the list to Laini.

1. How can we be sure you will clean up after a pet when you don't even keep your own room clean?

"They've got a point," said Laini, tossing the ball from one hand to another.

"Whose side are you on?" I asked. "Besides, my room is clean enough. It's just a *little* messy. The messiness helps me to be creative. What do they call it? A creative muse?"

"Well, unless your muse is going to get you a pet," said Laini, "you might want to straighten up your room a bit."

"I guess that one would be pretty easy to take care of," I said.

"Okay, so moving on," said Laini. "What's number two?"

2. A pet would be a distraction from your homework.

"That one's not fair. I always do my homework. Just maybe not right away," I said. "And school doesn't start again until September. That means I'll have to wait until then to even try to show them that I'll do my homework as soon as I get home. It will take forever to get a pet."

"Start doing some homeworky kind of things now. Read a lot, and maybe write some stuff. That'll make you look homework-ready."

It's good to have a best friend who knows how to strategize.

"Okay, then, next one," I said.

3. Getting a pet is a long-term decision, and we're not sure you're ready to make that kind of commitment.

"I've kept them as my parents all of my life. That's a huge commitment," I said.

"I don't know if they would see it that way," said Laini.

"Okay, so how about the fact that I've kept you as a friend since kindergarten? That's commitment."

"That could work," said Laini as she tried to spin the basketball on her finger. "What's next?"

4. Pets cost money. You don't have any.

Laini nodded and pointed at me. "They got you there."

"They kinda do," I said. "But I could start saving my allowance. And maybe I could earn some money."

"I could help you earn some," said Laini. "After all, it would kind of be like my pet, too. Except it would live here and you would take care of it. But I would come over and play with it."

"Sounds fair enough" is what I said out loud. Inside my head, I said, *I wish that's how it was going to happen.* A secret I had overheard told me things were going to be different.

I made myself focus on the last item on the list.

5. You need to show you can be responsible first.

"If I can take care of the first four items, then that means I'm responsible, right?" I said to Laini.

"Very responsible."

"But this is going to be hard."

"Well, maybe you could come up with your own list instead," said Laini.

"My own list of reasons I shouldn't get a pet?" I asked. That was a bizarre idea.

"Come on, Rica, get your head in the game. You need a list of reasons why you *should* get a pet—but a list written from *their* point of view."

Like I said, it's good to have a friend who knows how to strategize.

"It's time for us to get to work," said Laini. "This is going to be fun."

"Sure will" is what I said out loud.

*It better be* is what I said in my head since it could be the last thing Laini and I would ever get to do together.

Earlier in the week, I had heard Laini's mom talking—kind of whispering actually—on the phone. I had just gotten to their house and was still in the driveway when she walked out onto their side porch. I heard her say that she was glad they had finally found a house in Florida, just down the street from Grandma Shanahan's new condo. I peeked around the corner of the house and saw that she had a big smile on her face. She said that Laini and her brother, Quinn, were going to be thrilled and that she and their dad were trying to decide the perfect time to tell them.

My best friend was moving. Moving! And I couldn't tell her because I wasn't supposed to know.

I'm not very good at making new friends, and until then I hadn't needed to be. I had Laini. Being friends with her was easy-breezy, but now she was moving, and I had an icky-sicky feeling way down in the pit of my stomach. It felt like a giant knot of loneliness, and Laini hadn't even moved yet.

So, Laini moving to a whole other state was the real reason I wanted a pet. Actually, I didn't just *want* a pet. I *needed* a pet.

# TWO
# Plan A and Plan B

I was glad to catch Dad before he went to work. I only had two things on my Why I Should Get a Pet list, but I figured I could start trying them out.

"So, I've been thinking," I said. "I need to learn to be more responsible. Having a pet would teach me responsibility."

Dad gave me one of his big, wide smiles and said, "I hate to shoot your idea down, but that's putting the cart before the horse, so I think you're back to square one."

I wasn't exactly sure what he was saying, but it sounded like no.

"How does my bow tie look?" asked Dad as he straightened it in the hallway mirror.

"Like a bow tie," I answered.

"Good," he said. "That's what I was shooting for. I'm going to audition for this fall's community theater production after work and I want to look my best." He kissed me on the forehead and then, waving as he ran out the door, called out "Te logu!"

"Sure," I said. "See you later."

That didn't work out so well, so I moved on to Plan B: Momma.

I went down to the kitchen and poured myself

some cereal before my mother made me something I didn't want to eat for breakfast.

"So, I've been thinking," I told my mother. "I should get a pet because *you* really need one."

"I think I'm missing your logic," my mother said as she put a pot on the stove. She's a nutritionist. She writes cookbooks, makes recipe videos, and visits schools to talk about healthy eating. And she makes Dad and me eat healthy food that neither of us wants to eat.

"Dad's at work all day, and when summer's over, I go back to school. Since you work from home a lot, you'll be here by yourself." I crossed my fingers, hoping that this would work. "A pet would keep you company. It would be good for you."

"Sorry, that's not going to work, honey. I'm just fine by myself."

I tried again: "But I don't want you to be lonely."

"I've got too much work to do to be lonely." She gave me a smile. "But nice try."

I wasn't ready to give up.

"You don't even have to think of a name for it. I already have one picked out," I said. "Frederica. I'm giving away my name, so I can just be Rica."

"Don't you remember why you're named Frederica?" asked Momma.

"Because of some guy I never met," I answered.

"What do you mean 'some guy'?" asked Momma. "You're named after your great-great-grandfather Frederico. Don't you remember that all of your great-great-grandparents left Cape Verde for America because of all of the droughts? No rain meant no food, so people were starving.

Great-Great-Grandpa Frederico didn't forget Cape Verde after he left. He collected food and clothes to send back to the islands many times. A lot of people depended on those shipments. Always be proud of your name and your heritage."

I wasn't sure what *heritage* meant, but I figured it had something to do with Great-Great-Grandpa Frederico. I'm sure he was a terrific guy, but didn't I have a great-great-grand*mother* they could have named me after?

Momma took a box of brown rice out of the cabinet and told me she was going to make canja, a Cape Verdean chicken soup. "This version will be little healthier than the traditional recipe," she said. "I'm going to do a series of videos on African foods, so why not start with Cabo Verde?"

I liked canja the plain, old regular way, but I decided to keep that opinion to myself.

"Why do you call it Cape Verde sometimes and Cabo Verde other times?" I asked Momma.

"I grew up calling it Cape Verde, but then the country changed its name," answered Momma.

"So, I guess we're Cape Cabo Verdean."

Momma laughed. "Well, we're American, but I guess you could say we have Cape Cabo Verdean love in our blood."

"Cabo might be a cute pet name," I said.

Momma ignored my comment. "By the way, Tia Camille will be here in a little while to help me with a video. Serenity will be here, too."

"Oh, garbanzo beans!" I said.

"First of all," said Momma, "why do you always say 'garbanzo beans' when you're not happy with something? Garbanzo beans are just chickpeas. They're used to make hummus, and you like hummus."

Inside my head, I said, *I eat hummus, but I never said I like hummus.*

"Second of all," said Momma, "what is the problem you have lately with Serenity? She's your cousin, and you know you love her."

Inside my head, I said, *She's my cousin, so I probably do love her, but that doesn't mean I have to like her.*

"I think it would be good for you and Serenity to spend more time together," said Momma.

Out loud I repeated, "Oh, garbanzo beans!"

Momma gave me a warning look, so I started backing out of the kitchen. "Um, I think I'll go clean my room."

I've always been happy to see Momma's sister, Tia Camille, but lately Serenity had become the worst cousin in the world. Maybe fourteen is just the worst age, because, for some reason, she decided it was her job to tell me what to do and how to do it. People should wait until their kids are older before they name them because she definitely should not have been named Serenity. I wondered if I was going to be like her when I turned fourteen.

# THREE
## Serenity (Not)

Cleaning my room turned out to be a lot harder than it looked. First of all, where was I supposed to start? After staring at my room for about five minutes, I walked over to my desk and picked up my microscope. It was a little kid toy microscope and I hadn't used it in a while . . . but it looked kind of homeworky, so I put it back.

I picked up a collection of little yarn dolls from my dresser. I could get rid of them, but I made them when I was five and that was three years ago. Maybe keeping them showed commitment, so I put them back.

My glitter pens—purple, green, orange, pink, and blue—were all on the floor, so I put them on my desk. That was some kind of progress, right?

When I heard the back door open, I thought about hiding under the bed or in the closet, but there was no room. Maybe I should have cleaned a hiding place first. Before I had a chance to figure out a place to hide, Serenity (Not) was standing at my bedroom door. I made a face. Serenity *and* cleaning my room was too much to deal with at one time.

Serenity raised her eyebrows when she saw the face I made. "So, Miss Rica, what's got you in a bad mood?" she asked in a voice that sounded like she didn't really care.

"Maybe I'm trying to be more like you," I said in a fake sweet voice.

"My mood is perfectly fine with me," she said, pointing at herself. And then pointing that same long brown finger, nail perfectly polished, at me, she added, "And *your* mood is not my fault."

Serenity always has a quick answer for every-thing. I kind of want to be like her and kind of don't.

"What finally inspired you to clean your room?" she asked as she moved some things so she could make herself comfortable on my bed. "Not that you've gotten very far."

"I'm trying to show I'm responsible so I can get a pet," I answered.

"You know a pet is a lot of work, right?" said Serenity.

"Maybe," I said.

"You should consider a goldfish. You know, something you can handle."

Inside my head, I said, *I'm considering a lion so when you come to my door, it will ROAR and make you run.* Out loud I said, "I'm thinking of a baby llama."

"Baby llamas grow up to be big llamas."

I ignored her, picked up my lucky shirt from the chair, and put it into the hamper to be washed. It's always good to have your lucky shirt clean and ready to wear, although I've worn it dirty in a pinch.

Looking at her phone, Serenity called out, "This site recommends people get two llamas, never one. They're herd animals. Very social."

I really didn't want to have this conversation with Serenity anymore, so I was grateful when Laini showed up.

"It's the checkerboard friends," Serenity said as soon as Laini walked into the bedroom. She always calls us the checkerboard friends because we're "Black and White and always right next to each other." At first, we got kind of mad, but then we decided we were okay with it. But what would happen when Laini moved? If we couldn't be right next to each other, we wouldn't be the checkerboard friends anymore.

Laini waved at Serenity and then turned to me. "Your mother said you were cleaning your room. The list of reasons you should get a pet must not have worked out so well."

"I tried one reason on my father and another on my mother, but no luck."

"Cleaning your room is a good backup choice." She looked around. "Doesn't look like you've gotten very far, though."

Still looking at her phone, Serenity called out

again: "You'd have to get a barn or at least a really big shed for llamas. Your backyard is not that big."

I put my hands over my ears. "I can't hear you. I can't hear you."

Laini moved my hands away. "You can't clean your room with your hands over your ears, and I bet you won't get *any* kind of pet if you don't clean your room."

Laini is very logical.

"Oh, and they're kind of expensive," said Serenity. I prayed her phone would run out of battery soon. "You'll need money to buy a pet. Do you have any money?"

"Well, not yet," I said.

"Hmmm," she said. "I think I have a plan."

I needed a plan . . . but I wasn't so sure I needed one from Serenity.

"My cross-country team is having a cookout next weekend," said Serenity. "I really want to go. It will be my first chance to meet the whole team." Serenity had run cross-country in middle school, but this fall she would be in high school and that meant being on a new team. "But the Dangerous Duo are having a birthday party at the same time as the cookout and my mother wants me to help." The Dangerous Duo are Serenity's twin brothers, Jonah and Noah, who were turning five. "Maybe I could convince my mother to hire you. That way you make some money and I can go to the cookout."

"Well, shouldn't *you* pay us since you're the one who wants to go to the cookout?" I asked.

"That's not going to happen," said Serenity. "So . . . do you want to try this plan or not?"

It did sound like a pretty good plan. *If* we could convince our mothers.


"No." My mother wasted no time in shooting down our idea. "You can help. You *should* help. But you're not charging family."

"I'm not family," piped up Laini. Then she turned to me and whispered, "I could give the money I make to you."

"Sorry, Laini," Momma said. "Anyone who eats at my kitchen table as much as you do is family."

Laini actually likes my mother's food, so she eats over whenever she can.

"Hold on, Marissa," said Tia Camille. "I'm really going to need the extra help. I'm really, really going to need the extra help. Since the twins are turning five, I told them they could invite five friends. I meant five total, but they took it as five each. They had already told their friends, so I didn't have the heart to tell them no."

"There will be *ten* five-year-olds at the party?" My mother's eyes got big. "I told you I could cancel my plans to help."

"There will be twelve five-year-olds, including the twins. *Twelve!*" Tia Camille looked tired already. "But I don't want you to cancel your plans. And I do want Serenity to go to the team cookout."

"What about Will?" asked Momma. Uncle Will and Tia Camille aren't married anymore, but he still spends lots of time with Serenity and the twins.

"He's coming to help, but he'll need to drop off and pick up Serenity, so he won't be there the entire time. I'm hoping that a few of the other parents will stay, but I can't depend on it. Listen, I don't mind paying Rica and Laini. In fact, I'm sure I can't ever pay them enough."

"Thank you, Tia Camille! All we need is enough to buy a kinkajou. Or maybe a wallaroo. Can wallaroos live in this climate?" I wondered out loud.

WALLAROO

KINKAJOU

"You're not inspiring me to say yes," said Momma.

"Just kidding," I said quickly. "I don't really want a wallaroo. At least I don't think I want a wallaroo."

"Is it even legal to own a wallaroo?" asked Laini.

"Kinkajous are nocturnal, so they're up all night." Serenity was lightning fast at looking things up on her phone. "I'll check on wallaroos."

Momma closed her eyes and shook her head. "No. Please don't."

Finally, Momma said okay to us helping with the party. "But you head over there right after church and you help with everything," she said. "Setup, the party, and cleanup. Everything."

"Absolutely," I said.

"Start to finish," Laini said.

Serenity admired her perfect blue nails. "And I'll be at my cookout."

# FOUR
# Please and Thank You

That night, I took out my prayer journal. When I was little, I thought it would be hard for God to hear everyone's bedtime prayers at once, so as soon as I learned how, I started writing my prayers down to make it a little easier. Now I know that God can hear everything at the same time, but I guess I got used to writing my prayers down. I say thank you for something and then I ask for something. I figure that's fair.

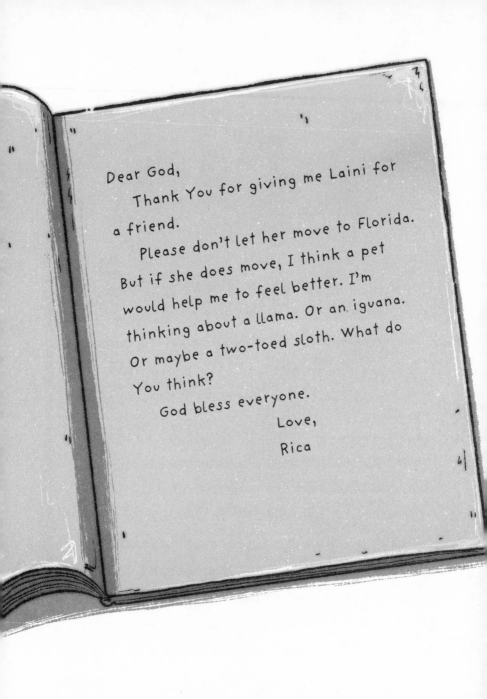

Dear God,

Thank You for giving me Laini for a friend.

Please don't let her move to Florida. But if she does move, I think a pet would help me to feel better. I'm thinking about a llama. Or an iguana. Or maybe a two-toed sloth. What do You think?

God bless everyone.

Love,

Rica

# FIVE
## Birthday Party Assistants Extraordinaire

**O**n the day of the party, Laini and I walked to Tia Camille's house.

"Think about it," I said. "We can make tons of money working little kids' birthday parties. We can call ourselves the Birthday Party Assistants Extraordinaire." Laini was planning to give her share of any money we earned to me for a pet, but I was planning to give it back to her when she moved to Florida. Since she wouldn't be around to enjoy the pet, that seemed fair.

"What parent wouldn't want help with their kid's birthday party?" said Laini.

"We can make flyers and put them up next to the preschool," I said.

"And we'll ask our parents to tell everyone they know," said Laini.

"We are strategizing geniuses!" I said as we high-fived each other.

When Tia Camille answered the door, I announced, "The Birthday Party Assistants Extraordinaire are here!"

"At your service," added Laini.

"Thank goodness," said Tia Camille. "I really need the two of you to play with the twins while I finish setting up."

"But the Birthday Party Assistants Extraordinaire are experts at setting up," I said.

"I'm sure that's true, but they delivered the bouncy house and Jonah and Noah have been aching to get in," said Tia Camille. "I told them they had to wait until the two of you got here."

Bouncy house? I love a good bouncy house. This birthday party thing was going to be even better than I'd thought.

The Dangerous Duo started jumping, flipping,

and screaming as soon as they got into the bouncy house. I got the feeling that I should have put my lucky shirt in the hamper sooner so that it would have been clean for the party. I was wearing my backup lucky shirt, but I wasn't sure if it was going to be enough.

"Careful, Jonah!" I yelled.
"I'm Noah!" He laughed.
"Then careful, Noah," I said.

"No, *I'm* Noah," said the other twin.

The twins love playing the who's who game. Even though I've known them all their lives, they still manage to fool me.

"Okay, you in the green shirt, careful." That solved that problem.

"Blue Shirt Twin, no pushing your brother!" yelled Laini. Then she turned to me. "*How* many kids are coming?"

"Twelve," I said. "Twelve little kids in a bouncy house." Maybe I didn't like bouncy houses so much.

Laini and I were already tired from watching Jonah and Noah when the other kids started arriving. I went over to the deck to get a few juice boxes to try to lure the twins out of the bouncy house so they could say hi to their friends.

A dad walked onto the deck and said, "I'm Mr. Hernandez. And that's my son Angel."

All I saw of Angel was the back of him, since he was already running into the bouncy house. I made a mental note: *Angel: striped shirt.*

"Be good, Lily," I heard a mom call out to her daughter, who ran into the bouncy house even faster than Angel had. *Pink shirt and really fast,* I noted to myself. I didn't even get a chance to see her face. Tia Camille was talking to a woman and a little girl wearing a long, frilly skirt. Tia Camille pointed at me. The little girl shook her head. I walked over to them.

"This is Mrs. Rivera and her daughter Reina," Tia Camille said. "They're new in the neighborhood. I asked Reina if she would let you bring her over to the other kids, but she said she's not ready."

"Are you sure?" I asked. "You can go into the bouncy house or play with the giant bubble wand."

Reina reached out and held her mother's hand. She held her head up high but did not budge.

Jonah stuck his head out of the bouncy house. "Lily knocked me down."

"I need backup over here!" yelled Laini from the bouncy house.

"I gotta go," I said to Reina. "Let me know if you change your mind." Then I ran to help Laini.

There were three kids in the bouncy house that I hadn't even seen come in.

"Watch out for Spider-Man Shirt," said Laini. "He keeps trying to climb up the sides. And Giraffe Shirt doesn't want anyone jumping near her, so of course Pink Shirt keeps jumping as close to her as she can."

"Only five kids in the bouncy house at a time!" I yelled.

No one got out. They didn't even look my way.

"Oh, garbanzo beans."

I needed a different idea. I looked around and saw the bubble wand. "Look! A giant bubble wand. I wonder if it's magic."

All the kids came running out of the bouncy house in a great big giant tangle. That wasn't quite my plan.

Luckily, Uncle Will was back from dropping off Serenity. He screamed like a monster and waved his arms in the air.

"There's a monster in the bouncy house!" he yelled as he jumped in.

Half the kids ran back into the bouncy house after him and started acting like they were monsters, too. The other half of them ran away from the bouncy house to the other side of the yard.

"It's okay," I told them. "The bubbles will scare the monsters away."

As we made giant bubbles, a few more kids arrived. I counted to see if everyone was there. Eleven plus the twins. Thirteen. I had a feeling that Reina had been added at the last minute. Tia Camille must have invited her because she was new.

Tia Camille brought pizza over to the picnic table. "See if you can get them to sit and eat," she said.

"No problem," I said out loud. Inside my head, I said, *And then I'll go and milk some chickens since I'll have had some practice doing the impossible.*

It took me, Laini, Uncle Will, and Mr. Hernandez to get them all to sit.

"I need ketchup," said Pink Shirt, whose name I had forgotten already.

"But you're having pizza," I said.

"I need ketchup on my pizza," Pink Shirt said.

"I'll get ketchup," said Tia Camille with a sigh.

Tia Camille came back with the ketchup. Pink Shirt picked up the squeeze bottle and pointed it at me.

"What are you doing?" I asked.

She smiled and took aim.

I was wiping the ketchup from my backup lucky shirt when the boy across from Pink Shirt lunged across the table to take the ketchup bottle from her. "My turn," he said with a grin.

"Oh, no, you don't, Baseball Jersey." Laini swiped the bottle from him.

"Jackson!" called out Baseball Jersey's dad from the deck. "Cut it out or no cake!"

When I heard "no cake," a brilliant idea dropped into my head. "You have to play the quiet game if you want cake," I told the kids. "No talking while you eat your pizza. Whoever is quiet the longest gets an extra piece of cake."

"There's a chocolate cake *and* a vanilla cake," said Blue Shirt Twin.

"Quiet means no talking, Blue Shirt Birthday Boy," said Laini. "One, two, three . . . quiet."

It actually worked. They sat without talking while they ate their pizza. Whenever one of them looked like they were getting antsy, Laini and I would just yell, "Cake!" It was like a magic word.

Tia Camille must have convinced Reina that it was okay to join the other kids, because she brought her over to the picnic table and handed her a slice of pizza. Reina took the pizza and gave Tia a smile but said nothing. She was already good at the quiet game.

"This is Reina," Tia Camille told everyone.

"Hi, Reina!" said Green and Blue Shirt Birthday Boys together.

"What's up, Reina?" said Striped Shirt.

"Hello, Reina," said Giraffe Shirt.

"Want ketchup, Reina?" asked Baseball Jersey.

Well, the quiet game was nice while it lasted.

# SIX
# Brainstorming

The deal was that we would stay to clean up, so we did. But I think a better name for the cleanup would have been disaster relief. We picked up toys, swept cake crumbs off of the deck, and wiped up blue and green frosting, which was *everywhere*.

When Serenity came back from her cookout, she saw us cleaning, gave us a smirk, and then plopped herself onto a deck chair. And, of course, she took out her phone.

Her smirk would have normally annoyed me, but I was too busy trying to decide what kind of pet to get now that Laini and I had actually started earning money.

"I'm thinking about a quokka," I told Laini.

"I've never heard of a quokka," she said.

"They're from Australia. You should see them. They look like they're actually smiling!"

"No go," said Serenity, looking at her phone. "Says here that they're a protected species."

She continued to scroll through her phone until Tia Camille came out, handed her a dishcloth, and pointed at the ketchup all over the picnic table.

I gave Serenity a nice big quokka-like grin.

Tia Camille paid us more than what she said she would.

"You don't have to give us extra," I said.

"Trust me, you earned it," she said. Then she gave us two of the ice cream shop certificates left over from the party giveaways. "Do you want Serenity to walk you there?"

"No, thank you," I said. This day had been hard enough already.

"We're good," Laini said.

"Okay," Tia Camille said. "But stop here on your way back so that I know you're okay."

"Deal," I said.

When we cut through the Delgados' yard, Laini picked up their basketball, made a quick basket in their driveway hoop, and then passed the ball to me. "No, thanks," I said. "I'd rather not miss and break their window."

She jumped again like she was trying to dunk, even though she wasn't nearly tall enough.

"It'll happen someday," I told her.

We turned down Main Street toward the ice cream shop. "That party was about the hardest work I've ever done in my life," I said.

"You and me both," said Laini. "There were a million of them—a million wild little monsters. They were cute, but a cute monster is still a monster."

"Except Reina. We probably should have tried harder to make sure she was having fun."

"Um, think about it," said Laini. "We were just trying to get out of there alive."

"And we succeeded, I think," I said, giving Laini a fist bump. "But I don't know about our Birthday Party Assistants Extraordinaire idea."

"Yeah, maybe not," said Laini. "I think it's time for Plan B."

"What's Plan B?" I asked.

"I have no idea," she said.

"We need to put our heads together," I said.

At the same time, we leaned our heads against each other's. And we laughed. Which made it hard to walk and still keep our heads together. We must have looked pretty silly, so, of course, who saw us walking into the ice cream store? My neighbor Mr. Fermino. He lives next door, and back when I was little, he was my first-grade teacher. The thing I remember most from first grade was him always saying, "You never know if a thing will work until you try." He was right. I told him I couldn't write poems, but by the end of the year, I ended up being pretty good at it.

Mr. Fermino looked at us but didn't say a word.

"Hi, Mr. Fermino," we said without separating our heads.

He took off his baseball cap and scratched his head, still not saying a word.

"We're putting our heads together because we need to come up with a good idea to help us make money so that I can get a pet," I said.

"Well, I guess that's one way to do it." He took a sip of his milkshake and said, "Or you could try brainstorming some ideas."

"Hey, I remember learning about brainstorming when you were my teacher," I told him.

"That's when you come up with a whole bunch of ideas, then pick the best one, right?" asked Laini.

"Yup," I answered. "You just keep thinking up ideas without worrying about how wacky they are."

Mr. Fermino nodded slowly and said, "Somehow I think you two can manage that."

"Yes, we can," said Laini, lifting her head.

"Absolutely," I said.

After we got our ice cream cones, we started brainstorming.

"What ideas do you have?" I asked Laini.

"None. You?" she asked.

"Got nothing," I said.

Mr. Fermino was sitting at the counter. "Look

around. You might see something to help you come up with an idea."

I looked out the window and saw Brendan Duncan walking his dog.

"A dog wash! We could have a dog wash!"

"That's a great idea," said Laini. "We'll need soap."

"And a tub or a bucket," I said.

"And a hose," she added.

Brendan's dog, who was almost as big as he was, saw another dog and started pulling Brendan down the street. Brendan could barely hold on to the leash.

"Maybe not a dog wash," I said.

"Yeah, maybe not," Laini agreed. "How about a car wash? My brother's baseball team had one last year. I think they made a lot of money."

"But they're a whole team. There are just two of us."

"True," Laini said. "How about raking leaves?"

"That wouldn't be until October. I don't want to wait that long to get a pet."

Mr. Fermino cleared his throat. When we looked

up, he said. "When you brainstorm, you don't shoot down the ideas. You just keep going with the list."

"Oh, yeah," I said.

"Dog walking!" said Laini.

"Backyard doggie poop cleanup!" I said.

"I draw the line," said Laini. "No backyard doggie poop cleanup."

"No shooting ideas down, remember?" Then I whispered, "But you're probably right. No backyard doggie poop cleanup."

"You know," Mr. Fermino said, "if you're trying to make money, the bookstore has a poetry contest going on. Fifty dollars for the winning poem."

"Fifty dollars!" Laini and I said at the same time.

"That's first place. Thirty dollars for second place. Ten dollars for third. You submit your poem to the bookstore by Wednesday. Then they pick out the finalists."

"Your poems are pretty good," Laini said to me. "Rica, I think you could win."

Ever since Mr. Fermino had told me I was good at writing poems, I'd written a lot of them. And put them in my bureau drawer. I had let Mr. Fermino and Laini read a few of them, but no one else. I didn't even let Momma and Dad know, since they would probably make me read some out loud in front of my grandparents, aunts, uncles, and cousins at our next family dinner.

"I think we should keep brainstorming ideas," I said.

"But fifty dollars, Rica," said Laini. Then she said it slowly. "Fif-ty dol-lars."

"I think we should keep brainstorming ideas," I repeated.

"Okay," said Laini. "I get it."

It's good to have a best friend who knows you well.

"Brainstorming caps back on," I said. I wondered if I could brainstorm ideas to keep her from moving.

"Let's focus," said Laini. "We could make jewelry and sell it."

"We could sell personalized greeting cards," I said.

"Custom-designed bookmarks."

"A lemonade stand!"

"A yard sale!"

"All of those!" I shouted. People in the ice cream shop looked at me funny, so I quieted down. "We could have a stand to sell lemonade, personalized cards, and jewelry personally designed by us. We could do all of it!"

"You could even sell some stuff from your room to help you clean it out. A Yard Sale Extraordinaire!"

"Sponsored by the Checkerboard Company!" I didn't mean to shout again, but I did.

"I think this plan will work," said Laini.

"Maybe I'll get a potbellied pig," I said.

Mr. Fermino turned around to look at me when I said "potbellied pig." "You know, you could bring home a little piglet but end up with a huge pig living in your house."

I wondered if he had been talking to Serenity.

# SEVEN
## One More Thing

Before I went to sleep, I decided to brainstorm a list of how I could get Laini and her family to stay. I took out a glitter pen, but then decided to use a permanent marker. It looked more like I meant business. I began my numbered list:

1.

But I put my marker down before even filling out the first item on the list. What if Laini would be excited about moving when she found out? After all, her grandma Shanahan was moving to Florida, too. Plus Florida had warm weather, palm trees, and beaches that you could go to in January. She would probably like Florida. Maybe it wouldn't be fair to try to make my best friend stay if she might be happier there. I took out my prayer journal instead.

Dear God,

Thank You for letting Laini and me survive the birthday party.

Please help our yard sale extraordinaire be much easier than the party was.

And one more thing . . . I just asked You for something, so I know I shouldn't ask You for anything else, but I'm kind of desperate right now. If Laini moves, please teach me how to make new friends, because I really have no idea. And, even if I do make new ones, none of them would be Laini, so maybe getting a pet is better. Please?

God bless everybody.

Love,

Rica

# EIGHT
# Sponsored by the Checkerboard Company

We used the money from our birthday party earnings to buy supplies for the Yard Sale Extraordinaire. We called it an investment. We tried to convince my parents to invest in our yard sale, too, and they finally gave us five dollars. They called it a loan.

We decorated the yard with streamers and ribbons. Mr. Fermino lent us a folding table for the yard sale items. We wanted to make a huge Yard Sale Extraordinaire sign to hang on the table.

"Maybe we can find something in my room that we can use," I said.

"Good luck with that," said Laini.

My mother snickered. "Where did your dad go? He's missing a perfect opportunity to make a comment about a needle in a haystack."

We went into the house and searched my entire room but came up with nothing.

I gave the globe on my desk a spin. Then I counted the states between Massachusetts and Florida.

"You're not putting your globe in the yard sale, are you?" asked Laini. "Globes are kind of cool."

"I think this one is too big," I told her. "Way too big."

I thought again about telling her what I'd heard. But if she didn't want to move, it would make her sad to find out. And if she did want to move . . . well, that would make *me* even sadder than I already was.

Momma peeked her head into my room. "You're in luck. Tia Camille has a big roll of paper that you can use to make a banner."

"Great!" I said.

"Serenity is on her way over with it," Momma said. "She should be here in a few minutes."

"Thanks" is what I said out loud. Inside my head, I said, *I'd rather write* Yard Sale Extraordinaire *on my forehead with a permanent marker.*

"You're turning into quite the business person. Just like Great-Great-Grandpa Frederico," Momma said.

"Thanks" is what I said out loud again. Inside

my head, I said, *But I'm probably still giving away my name.*

When Serenity arrived with the roll of paper, we didn't turn it down. Laini carefully wrote *Yard Sale Extraordinaire!* in big colorful letters. I added *Sponsored by the Checkerboard Company.* Serenity leaned against the light post and scrolled through her phone.

Laini and I taped the banner to the front of the table, trying to make it as straight as we could. Serenity didn't even look up.

"Thanks for the help," I said to Serenity.

She rolled her eyes and looked back at her phone.

"I hope this yard sale works," I said.

"Well," said Laini, "if it doesn't, you might want to think about the poetry contest."

Serenity looked up from her phone. "Poetry contest?"

I looked at Laini like she had eighty-eight heads. Why in the world would she mention the poetry contest in front of Serenity?

"Tell me about this poetry contest," said Serenity.

"I'm pretty sure it's over. Too late. Oh, well, next time." I tried to change the subject. "So, Serenity, are you looking forward to high school? I'm sure that will be exciting."

Serenity tilted her head, raised her eyebrows, and made her lips crooked. Even though she hadn't said anything, I could almost hear the words *Don't*

*bother trying to change the subject* come out of her mouth.

"Tell me about this poetry contest," Serenity repeated. "Which I'm willing to bet is *not* over."

"The bookstore is having a poetry contest," I confessed. "And, no, I'm not entering it."

"What would you get for winning this contest?" she asked.

"I'm not entering it," I said.

"Would you win money? Don't you need money for a pet?"

"I'm not entering it."

Serenity was very good at making arguments go her way, so the less I said, the better.

"Well," she said, "I don't know how good your poetry writing skills are, but to win, they would have to be pretty good. I have a few ideas for you . . ."

Before she could get another word out, I repeated, "I'm. Not. Entering. The. Contest."

Serenity shook her head, rolled her eyes, and then started walking home. Maybe she meant to wave goodbye, but the way she flicked her hand it looked more like she was saying *I'm through with you*.

If only.

# NINE
## Yard Sale Extraordinaire

We had our banner, streamers, and ribbons. We had markers, stickers, and glitter to personalize our greeting cards. We had a ton of yard sale items. We had everything.

Everything but customers.

We waited for the crowds to show up. Nobody came. I wondered if I was going to have to start writing a poem.

"I wish we had phones," said Laini. "Then we could post something online to get people to come by. Maybe we could ask your parents."

"Maybe. But if I do this without their help, it looks like I'm more responsible. Maybe we can ask your brother."

Laini shook her head. "Quinn's at an overnight baseball camp. He's trying to make sure I never get better than him, but I've been practicing my swing."

We looked around but nobody was headed our way, so we slumped down in our chairs. We waited some more until Laini sat up.

"Hey!" she said. "I know: maybe we can get Serenity to post something for us."

"Maybe there's *no way* I'm asking Serenity to help."

We slumped back down in our chairs.

Finally, I said, "Forget technology. We're going old school."

"Huh?" said Laini.

"My dad says that sometimes you have to go 'old school,'" I said. "Or as he says it, 'ol' skooool.' I think that means there are ways to get the word out without a phone."

We got paper, markers, tape, and chalk. First, we put up flyers. Then we drew chalk footsteps pointed in the direction of our stand around the entire block. On each corner, we wrote *Walk this way to the Yard Sale Extraordinaire.* We even put some flyers and footsteps near the ice cream shop.

"I bet this works," said Laini. "You are a strategizer extraordinaire."

"Maybe I'll get a two-toed sloth," I said.

We fist-bumped and headed back to my house.

Mr. Fermino came over with a speaker. "Some music might help."

"That's a good idea," I said.

"But if I'm going to have to listen to it all afternoon, let's play something I want to hear." He put on Cape Verdean music. "A little Kriolu music will have everyone in the neighborhood coming by."

I don't know if it was the music, the signs, or the sidewalk drawings, but a few people started showing up.

Then Tia Camille showed up with a whole bunch of people—the Wild Ones from the birthday party with some of their parents. In front of the pack was Lily on her bike.

"Well, hello, Pink Shirt," I said.

She looked down at her shirt. "It's purple."

"You'll always be Pink Shirt to me," I told her.

A boy in a football jersey gave us a big smile and asked, "Do you sell ketchup?" He might have had on a different jersey, but we would recognize him anywhere: Baseball Jersey.

"Absolutely not," said Laini.

"Not on your life," I added.

He looked disappointed but started looking around at the other things on the table. I immediately reached over and took the slime away. "Already sold," I told him.

"Smart move," said Baseball Jersey's dad.

One of the twins ran over to Laini. I think it was Jonah. No, it was Noah. No, actually it was Jonah. Maybe. Anyway, one half of the Dangerous Duo ran over to Laini and said, "Bet you don't know which one I am."

"Bet you're right," answered Laini.

"I told the birthday party parents that they owed you," Tia Camille whispered in my ear.

"You're my favorite aunt," I whispered back as I gave her a hug.

Tia Camille had brought Reina with her. "Do you remember Reina?" she asked me.

Even if she hadn't been wearing another long, frilly skirt, I would have remembered her. "Hi, Reina!"

Reina tugged on my T-shirt. "My name means 'queen,'" she said. She had a little bit of an accent.

"You're certainly dressed the part," I told her. "What are you queen of?"

She thought for a second and then quietly answered, "Me."

"Well," I said, "if you're going to be queen of something, yourself is probably a good thing to be queen of."

"If she gets to be a queen, do I get to be a king?" asked Spider-Man Shirt, who was now wearing a Superman shirt.

"Sure," I answered. "King of yourself."

"Yay!" Spider-Man Shirt turned to the other kids. "Hey, everybody, I am king of the kingdom of me!"

"I don't want to be a king," said Striped Shirt,

who was wearing a different striped shirt. "I want to be a zebra."

"Go ahead," Laini told him. "You do you."

Reina tugged at my T-shirt again.

"Do you sell crowns?" she asked.

Laini bent over to look her straight in the face and without even smirking said, "Aisle three."

Reina looked at Laini, waiting for a better answer.

I elbowed Laini and told Reina that we didn't have any crowns. Then I cut something that looked like a crown out of some poster paper. I handed it to Reina along with some glitter pens and stickers.

"You can make your own. No charge."

Reina worked on her crown while Laini and I sold more stuff. When she was done, she neatly put the glitter pens and the rest of the stickers back. Then she put her crown carefully on her head.

We sold three bracelets, two books, four cards, a stuffed dinosaur, and seven glasses of lemonade. I also gave away a soccer ball to a little boy named Francisco.

"Stop giving stuff away for free," Laini managed to both yell and whisper in my ear at the same time.

"Did you see the way his face lit up when he saw the soccer ball?"

Laini smacked her forehead with her hand and shook her head. "You're never gonna get a pet this way."

The Wild Ones were having fun playing hopscotch. First, they hopscotched one at a time. Then they all tried to jump it at the same time see who could do it the fastest. They tripped over one another, fell down, and laughed.

With her crown on her head, Reina shot baskets in the driveway. She didn't make a single one.

"She needs some coaching," I told Laini.

"Um, we're a bit busy with a yard sale right now," she answered. "Maybe tomorrow."

I collected money for one of my old puzzles but kept glancing at Reina. She still hadn't made a basket. She might have been worse than me at free throws, but she kept trying.

I hoped one of the other kids would go over to

play with her, but they were busy playing hopscotch. I left the yard sale table to walk over to Reina.

"Why don't you go over and play with them?" I asked Reina.

"They are kind of loud," she said. "I am not kind of loud."

She was right, but you shouldn't have to be loud to make friends.

"And they say I talk funny," she said.

"You talk with a little accent," I said. "I think they meant to say you talk differently from them, not that you talk funny." Reina smiled when I added, "And it sounds pretty."

I pointed at Giraffe Shirt, who was drawing with chalk on the sidewalk. "You could try playing with her."

Reina looked at Giraffe Shirt but didn't move.

"Three lemonades coming up!" I heard Laini yell. She looked at me and yelled again: "Is the cashier on break or something?"

Sometimes Laini could be a loud friend, but I was still going to miss her when she moved. A lot.

As I was collecting money for the lemonade, I heard a small voice say, "I can do this." I turned around and saw Reina smoothing her skirt and straightening her crown. Then she walked over to Giraffe Shirt and said, "Hi, can I play?"

*Wow*, I thought. *Who knew you could be brave just by deciding to be?*

When the yard sale was over, we counted up our money. We made $17.50. And since I was giving Laini her half of the money when she moved, that left me with $8.75.

"I don't think this is going to be enough for a hedgehog," I said. "But maybe I don't want a hedgehog anyway. They're not very cuddleable."

"Neither am I sometimes," said Laini.

Mr. Fermino came over to get his table. "Make any money?"

"Not enough," I said. "I'll never get a pet this way."

He took his wallet out of his pocket. "Why don't you give me that card over there," he said. "My sister in Ohio has a birthday coming up."

I handed the card to him.

"Obrigadu," he said.

"You're welcome," I answered. I wasn't sure if he even had a sister in Ohio. I think he was just trying to be nice. But at least we were up to $18.50.

We packed everything up.

Mr. Fermino folded up his table. "How badly do you want a pet?" he asked. "The poetry contest could be worth a try."

I scrunched up my face.

"Just something to think about," he said as he turned and headed home.

I could probably write a poem. I could definitely write a poem. I would just rather put it in my bureau drawer instead of entering it in the contest. But fifty dollars for the winner. Hmmm . . .

As if she had read my mind, Laini said, "You know, if you won the poetry contest, you would be a whole lot closer to getting a pet. You could get that llama. Or maybe a miniature pony."

"A baby pygmy goat." I had made my decision. I wanted a baby pygmy goat. "And maybe, *maybe*, for that I'll enter the contest."

# TEN
# A Whole Different Kettle of Fish

The next day, I picked out a notebook to write my poem in. Then I searched for the perfect pen. I decided on a green one, since green is the color of money and money was what I needed from this contest.

I sat down at my desk with my notebook, my green pen, and absolutely no words. Just a blank page staring at me. Even though I'm pretty good at writing poems, I was having no luck with this one. It was one thing to write one and put it in my drawer. Writing a poem that someone else was going to read was, as my dad would say, a whole different kettle of fish.

Writing the poem was so hard that I suddenly felt like cleaning my room instead. Where to start? Under my bed? My closet? My desk? I decided under my bed could wait because who could see it anyway? Same if I closed my closet door. My desk was covered with stuff. It was time to get rid of some things.

I decided whatever was in good shape could be donated to the church for the annual bazaar, so I took everything off of my desk and then sorted it into a donate pile, a toss pile, and a keep pile. When I finished, I had one thing in my donate pile, one thing in my toss pile, and everything else in my keep pile.

Cleaning my room was so hard that I suddenly felt like I should work on the poem. And since sitting at my desk and working on the poem seemed like a homeworky kind of thing, I made sure my bedroom door was wide open. That ended up being a mistake because guess who came walking in. I wondered if there was a way to install some kind of Serenity warning signal on the house.

"I really think you should enter the poetry

contest." Serenity came right up next to me and did a terrible job of pretending that she wasn't trying to peek at my notebook. I closed it and gave her the evil stare. But I should have known it wouldn't work on her because she kept right on talking.

"Are you working on your poem now? I just told your mother about the contest. She thinks it's a good idea."

"Oh, garbanzo beans."

"So, what's your poem going to be about?" she asked.

"Frogs," I answered. It wasn't but that was the quickest one word answer I could think of.

"Well, that's okay . . . if you're passionate about frogs," said Serenity. "Poems should reflect your passions."

Serenity was right. I could probably write a great poem about how passionately I wanted her to go home.

"What's your format?"

*Words,* I said to myself. *Words on paper.*

Serenity didn't care that I hadn't answered her question out loud. She just kept talking.

"You could write a sonnet. Fourteen lines. Very Shakespearean. Or a haiku. A haiku has three lines. The first line has five syllables, the second has seven syllables, and the last one has five. They're short, but not as easy to write as you think they would be."

Clearly, she was on a roll and there was no stopping her.

"Don't forget rap. And of course, there's always free verse."

I wondered if a person could ever use up all of

their words and just run out of things to say. I was pretty sure Serenity was close to her limit.

"But your topic is most important. It has to be something that really means something to you. You could write about important people in your life." Serenity stretched one of her curls out and let it pop back. "You know, like a role model." She tilted her head and smiled. "Someone you really look up to."

I got up, plopped myself onto my bed, and covered my head with my big stuffed yellow duck until she finally left.

I lifted my duck off of my head and peeked. I didn't see her anywhere. I listened closely. I didn't hear her anywhere. I figured it was safe to sit back at my desk and work on the poem. I wrote until dinnertime and then I wrote before I went to bed.

The next morning, I finished a draft of my poem, but it was pretty bad. I decided to take a break, so I got out a book to read. I read in the living room since I figured it would help my case if my mother walked by and saw me reading.

As soon as I sat on the couch, I heard the kitchen screen door open.

"Hi, Tia." It was Serenity's voice.

*Oh, garbanzo beans!* I said it only in my head because I didn't dare make a sound.

"What are you making?" Serenity asked my mother. "It smells delicious."

"I was trying out a new whole grain bread recipe. Smells good but it fell flat," I heard my mother say. "I'm going to have to give it another try."

"Call me if you need a taste tester," said Serenity.

"Thank you, sweetie," my mother answered. "Now if I could only get Rica to do the same."

"I'll work on her," said Serenity.

Add that to the list of reasons I spend way too much time thinking of how I can hide from Serenity.

"Is Rica around?" Serenity asked. "How is she doing with her poem?"

No way I was letting Serenity read my poem. I was not in the mood to listen to her tell me everything that was wrong with it, followed by her ideas of how to fix it.

I tiptoed to the front door, ran to the maple

75

tree, and, still holding my book, climbed as high as I dared. Sitting in the tree was one of my favorite places to read, so I was pretty good at climbing it with a book in my hand.

It was much cooler in the tree. I considered spending the rest of the summer in it. If I got some rope and hung a pail from the tree, I could ask my mother to put food in it and I could just haul it up.

On second thought, maybe I would ask my dad to put food in it.

Through the leaves, I could see Kiara, Rose, and Brooklyn walking by my house. I knew them and they knew me, but we weren't really friends. Maybe we could be friends when Laini moved. Kiara was one of the few Black girls in my class. People seemed to expect that we would be friends, and I wouldn't mind that, but what was I supposed to do, walk up to her and say "Hi, we're friends now"? That would be awkward. I got this sinking feeling that when Laini moved, I would be standing around feeling awkward a lot.

When I looked the other way, I saw Reina on a bike with her mother holding the back of it. It

looked like she was trying to learn how to ride without training wheels. When her mother let go, Reina wobbled but kept on riding. She rode a little more until she wobbled again and started to tip over. She put her foot on the ground to catch herself and got right back to riding. She was the absolute queen of trying.

From inside the house I could hear my mother and Serenity calling me. I wouldn't have said anything, except I figured my mother would start to get worried and call the police. The story would go viral and I'd forever be known as the missing kid. I could embarrass myself all by myself. I didn't need that kind of help.

Finally, I yelled, "I'm up here!"

"Where?" I could hear my mother yell back.

"Up here," I repeated.

Serenity walked outside and looked up. "I found her!" she yelled to my mother. "Why are you in the tree?" she asked. "Come down so you can show me what you wrote so far."

"Never," I answered.

"I just want to help you," she said.

"No. Way."

Serenity tilted her head and made a face. "Don't make me climb up there."

"You can climb up here," I said, "but you might break a nail."

Serenity looked at her green glitter polished nails. "You're probably right. But I don't know why you're so stubborn."

I showed her my teeth and pretended it was a smile. Then I opened my book and started to read.

"Why do I even bother to try?" asked Serenity. She started to walk away but then turned around and said, "You know I'll be back."

Yup, spending the rest of the summer in the tree was sounding like a great idea.

# ELEVEN
## Hoodwinked

It took that whole day and most of the next, but I finally came up with a poem that I kind of liked. Then I rewrote it, and rewrote it, and rewrote it again. And again. It was as ready as it was ever going to get.

"Honey, I can't go with you to the bookstore this morning," Momma said when I told her I was ready to drop off my poem. "I'm trying to take advantage of this break in the heat to work on my new bread recipe. It fell a bit flat last time, but I think I've got it figured out."

When she told me to call Serenity, I tried to convince her that I could walk the whole way by myself. She wasn't having it. Maybe she'll let me cross Main Street by myself by the time I'm thirty.

On my way to get Serenity, I saw Kiara again. This time she was walking with Aubrey. Kiara seemed nice, but Aubrey did not. Not at all. The only reason I could think that they were friends was that they had both moved into town at the start of third grade. New kid bonding, I guess.

When I walked by them, Kiara gave me a smile and said hi but Aubrey just looked at me as if to say *What are you looking at?* How was I supposed to make friends with that?

I said hi to Kiara but then kept walking because I didn't know what to say to Aubrey. At least I'd already be good at feeling awkward by the time Laini left.

Serenity was waiting for me on her front steps. Even though I had wanted to walk to the bookstore alone, I was kind of glad she was with me in case I ran into Kiara and Aubrey again.

That is, until she started talking.

"Do you want to read your poem to me?" asked Serenity.

*I'd rather eat brussels sprout pancakes,* I said in my head. Out loud I just said, "No."

"Do you want to win or not?" asked Serenity.

"Yes," I answered.

"Then read it to me. I can help," she said.

She was probably right. She probably could help me. But if I let her help, Miss Know-It-All would rewrite everything, and then it would be her poem and not mine.

"No," I answered.

"Okay, so *don't* win enough money to buy a pygmy goat or whatever it is that you want today," she said. "Getting a goat might not be good idea, anyway. They're really loud. And you have to find out if it's okay with the town to have one. And, just like llamas, they're social, so you really need to get two. But if you still want one, let me help you with your poem."

"No," I said again. Of all of the people in the entire world that I did not want to read my poem to, Serenity was on the top of the list.

"Do you know why I love running cross-country and track?" asked Serenity.

Even though I hadn't asked and didn't care, she decided to tell me anyway.

"There's a whole team who's with you. Your teammates are always challenging you to do your best. Want to run faster? Run with someone faster than you. Want to run farther? Run with someone who can run farther than you. The whole team is helping everyone to be their best."

I pretended to be interested in everything we were passing—the ice cream store, the library, the big tree in the park—but it didn't matter. She kept right on talking.

"Since I'm older, I've done more writing. Maybe I can give you ideas on how to make your poem even better."

"Oh, look. A bird," I said, pointing.

Serenity rolled her eyes. For one short, sweet moment, I thought she was going to stop talking. But then she opened her mouth again and talked all the way to the bookstore.

When we got there, I waited for the salesperson

to finish helping a customer while Serenity stayed at the front of the store, reading a sign on the bulletin board. But just as the salesperson was handing me an entry form, Serenity came running over.

"There was a form in front. I already filled it out for you," she said with a smile. "All you have to do is staple your poem to it."

I wasn't sure why she was being so nice, but I guess everyone has their moments. I took my poem out of my pocket, and Serenity grabbed it, stapled it to the form, and put it in the entry box.

"There," she said. "You're all set."

Something didn't seem quite right.

On the way out of the store, I saw the sign about the poetry contest on the bulletin board that Serenity had been reading. When I started reading it, Serenity tugged at me to leave.

"Wait a minute!" I said. "This says finalists have to read their poems *out loud* on Saturday. Here. In the bookstore. In front of people." I had been hoodwinked!

"You will do fine," said Serenity.

"That's why you filled out the form for me," I said. "No way I'm reading my poem out loud!"

"Quiet, before you make a scene." Serenity took my arm and headed out the door before I could finish reading the sign. "Come on," she said. "I'll buy you an ice cream."

Ice cream or no ice cream, Serenity was the worst cousin in the world.

# TWELVE
## Mixed Feelings

Dear God,

Please don't let the bookstore pick my poem.

Please let the bookstore pick my poem.

God, I don't mean to confuse You, but that's kind of exactly how I feel.

God bless everyone.

Love,

Rica

P.S. I forgot to tell You thank You for something. But I will. As soon as I think of something.

# THIRTEEN
## Try Anyway

I couldn't believe they chose my poem. I was a finalist! I did not at all want to read my poem out loud, but if I won fifty dollars, maybe I would be able to afford my baby pygmy goat. I was split between being terrified and excited . . . but terrified was winning.

Saturday came way too fast. I looked for my lucky shirt. My mother had washed it, but since I hadn't put my clothes in the drawer like she asked me to, it was kind of wrinkled. I smoothed it out as much as I could. It was still a little wrinkled, but I put it on anyway. Desperate times called for desperate measures.

Besides Momma and Dad, Tia Camille came to the bookstore with Serenity and the Dangerous Duo. Laini came with her mother. A few of the Wild Ones were there with their parents. Even Mr. Fermino came.

I think it would have been easier if no one came. I didn't feel like my lucky shirt was working. Maybe I shouldn't have let it get wrinkled.

After I checked to make sure my mother and father weren't looking, I started heading toward the door—the door and home.

"I know you don't think you're leaving." Serenity stood between me and the door. "You're going up there whether you like it or not."

The absolute worst cousin in the world. "I can't do it. Not in front of all these people. What if I get up there and no words come out?"

"Listen to me." Serenity put her hands on my shoulders, and with her face close to mine, she said softly, "I've known you since you were born. You're smart and you're talented. You got this. You hear me? I'll be right here. If you get scared, just look at me."

When they called my name, I just sat there, frozen, but Serenity kicked the back of my chair. When I turned around, she gave a look that told me I was going up there.

Even though I had memorized my poem, I looked at the paper instead of looking up. For a moment, just as I feared, no words came out. I heard someone clear their throat, and when I looked up, I saw Serenity smiling, nodding, and mouthing, *You got this.*

Serenity was the worst cousin in the world.

Except when she was the best.

I took a deep breath and read.

## ANYWAY

There can be no dunk without the jump.
No home run without swinging the bat.
If you want to give yourself the chance to rise,
You've got to risk falling flat.

There's no yes without asking the question.
No leading role without stepping onstage.
If you want to learn to ride, get on the bike.
If you want victory, get in the race.

Give it a try,
Even when you're afraid.
Trying is hard.
Try anyway.

I did it! I collapsed into a chair in relief and the rest of the readings went by in a blur. They announced the winners and I had won second place. Maybe next time, not that I would ever do this again, I would let someone look at my poem so I could make it even better. Then I could win first place.

But thirty dollars was better than no dollars! I was that much closer to getting a pet.

Momma and Dad gave me a big hug and told me they were proud of me.

Laini gave me a fist bump. "I bet you have enough for a baby pygmy goat now!"

Serenity walked over to me, put her hands on her hips, and said, "Let me get this right. You were going to leave without trying even though you wrote a great poem about *trying*?" She had a *How bizarre can you possibly be?* look on her face.

"Sometimes my bravery needs encouragement," I told her. I gave her a quick hug and said thank you.

I never thought I would see the day, but Serenity Conway was standing there speechless.

But when the bookstore judge handed me my prize, it wasn't the cash I was expecting.

Laini exclaimed, "It's a gift card?"

"Yeah," I said, whispering so I wouldn't hurt anyone's feelings. "And I don't think the bookstore sells baby pygmy goats."

"Well, you could buy some stuff here and we could sell it in another yard sale."

I wasn't quite sure I was up to that, so I was back to square one. But with everything I had learned about trying lately, I knew that being back at square one didn't mean I was giving up. It just meant I was starting over.

The Dangerous Duo came over with their band of Wild Ones. They gave me a great big group hug and then ran straight back to the kids' section. Except Reina. She looked up at me and stayed right by my side.

The poem wasn't just mine. Reina was the one who was really good at trying. It was after seeing how she was always willing to try that I started realizing how often other people around me were also willing to give something a try. The poem was hers, too.

I looked at the gift card and then walked her over to the picture book section. We picked out one picture book written in English and one in Spanish.

When we stood in line to pay, Reina smiled and waved Giraffe Shirt over. She reached out to hold Giraffe Shirt's hand, and then with her other hand, reached out to hold mine.

Some conversations don't even need words.

# FOURTEEN
## Clear the Shelters

Momma and Dad said they didn't know if they were prouder of my poem or that I used the gift card to buy books for Reina.

"You hit that ball out of the park with your poem," said Dad. "And you certainly went the extra mile when you used the card for Reina. I'm very proud of you."

"Great-Great-Grandpa Frederico was also a philanthropist," said Momma.

I wasn't sure what a philanthropist was, but Momma's smile told me it was a good thing.

"You earned more than the gift card today," said Momma. "You earned yourself the right to get a pet."

"Really?" I couldn't believe my ears. "I can finally get a pet?" I gave them a big hug.

"Well, first," said Momma, "we'll need to get everything it needs, so be thinking of what kind of pet you want."

"But no llamas," said Dad.

"Or wallaroos," said Momma.

"Well," I said, "how about a baby pygmy goa—?"

"No!" they said loudly. In unison, of course.

I went outside to shoot free throws while I tried to figure out how to convince my parents that a baby pygmy goat would be the perfect pet. Maybe once they saw how cute they were, they would change their minds.

Every shot I took hit the rim and bounced off. But hitting the rim was an improvement, so I kept trying.

"Keep your eye on the hoop, not the ball." Mr. Fermino was outside working on his garden. "Always look to where you want the ball to go, not where it is."

When I looked over, he tipped his hat and said, "Good job today."

"Thanks," I answered. "Did you know the prize was a bookstore gift card, not cash?"

"Maybe," he answered with a wink.

"Why didn't you tell me?" I asked.

"You never know if a thing will work until you try," he answered. "And if you knew the prize wasn't cash, would you have tried?"

*I should have known*, I thought.

"I think I still need money," I told him. "My parents said I could get a pet, but I was so excited, I didn't ask if that meant they were going to pay for it. But I kind of feel like I should pay for it."

"The animal shelter is participating in the Clear the Shelters program starting in late August," Mr. Fermino said. "But if you don't want to wait, right now they've got a lot of cats and kittens, way more than they can care for."

"For free?" I asked. "I can afford free."

"Well, almost free," he said. "Somebody made a big donation so the shelter could waive most of their fees and get these cats adopted. They just ask for a small donation from anyone who can afford it. Every little bit helps."

"Did you know that before you told me to enter the bookstore contest?" I asked.

"Maybe," he answered with another wink.

*Of course, he did,* I thought.

"Think they might be giving away pygmy goats anytime soon?" I asked him.

"I highly doubt it," Mr. Fermino said.

"Miniature donkeys?"

"Wouldn't bet on it."

"Toucans?"

Mr. Fermino just looked at me.

"I guess that's a no," I said.

"They have cats," he said. "Lots of cats."

"But they're almost free?"

"Almost."

"Hmmm . . ."

# FIFTEEN
## Exciting News

Dad stuck his head out the door. "Rica, Mr. and Mrs. Shanahan want you to head down to Laini's house. They have a surprise to tell you about."

Were they going to announce that they were moving to Florida? I tried to look surprised about the surprise since I wasn't supposed to know, but I don't think it worked too well.

"You don't look excited," said Dad.

"I guess I'll have to see what the surprise is first," I said.

I told Mr. Fermino thank you and headed over to Laini's house. Laini and I had walked to each other's houses a zillion times. I think we both could walk it with our eyes closed if we had to. When we were walking together, we would do a quick hopscotch over the tree roots that had pushed through the sidewalk. We would always remind each other to duck under the branches that hung down low. We knew the shady yards to cut through when it was hot and the sunny backyards to cut through when it was cold. I felt a big, empty hole growing inside me. I wouldn't need to remember any of this after Laini moved.

I wondered if Laini would be excited about me getting a pet if she knew she was going to move. I could send her pictures, but it wouldn't be the same. I wasn't even sure if I was completely excited. A pet might be good company after Laini left, but it wouldn't be Laini.

Kiara, Rose, and Brooklyn were walking across the street. I wished sometime I would see just one of them by themselves. It would be a lot easier than talking to all three of them. But they were never alone. I was the only one who was going to have to be alone.

In my head, I heard a small voice say, *I can do this*. It sounded like Reina's voice. Then I heard another voice say, *Trying is hard. Try anyway*. It was my voice. I took a deep breath, straightened my imaginary crown, and crossed the street to say hi to them.

It was easier than I thought it would be. I said hi and asked them if they had done anything fun this summer. Then they asked me if I had done anything fun this summer. Then they said we should do something fun together sometime this summer and I said sure.

I felt pretty good . . . well, for a minute. Then I got to Laini's house and remembered that my very best friend was moving away.

Mr. Shanahan answered the door with a big smile. "Rica, I hear you did a wonderful job reading your poem today."

"Thanks," I said, trying to look happy.

Mr. Shanahan called Laini and Quinn and then we all went into the kitchen. Mrs. Shanahan looked excited. I wondered if they really thought I was going to be happy about them moving. Laini sat down at the table, but I couldn't get my legs to bend so I just stayed standing.

"We have some exciting news," said Mrs. Shanahan.

I looked at Mrs. Shanahan and then at Mr. Shanahan. Then I looked at Laini. Tears started pouring down my face, and words started pouring out of my mouth.

"I already know the news and I'm sorry, Mrs. Shanahan, but I was in your driveway when you were on the porch talking on your phone and you didn't see me and I didn't mean to listen in but I was right there and I heard the whole conversation about you moving to Florida."

"We're moving?" Laini jumped up so fast that her chair fell over.

"What? We're moving?" yelled Quinn, looking as surprised as Laini.

"Wait. Who said we're moving?" Mr. Shanahan picked up Laini's chair. "We're not moving."

"We're going on vacation." Mrs. Shanahan stood up and put her arm around Laini. "To Florida."

Then she turned to me and wiped the tears from my face.

"You're not moving?" I said.

"We're not moving?" Laini said.

"So, we're *not* moving?" Quinn said.

"No," said Mr. Shanahan as he handed me a tissue. "We're renting a beach house in Florida during your winter school break and, Rica, we want you to come with us. Your family was nice enough to invite Laini when you went on vacation last February, and the two of you had so much fun that we thought we'd invite you to come with us."

Mrs. Shanahan added, "We already talked with your parents and they said it was fine with them. We weren't going to say anything for a while but decided it would be a good idea to make sure it was fine with you before we bought the airline tickets."

I felt like an idiot because I started crying all over again, and who cries when they're told they're going on a beach vacation with their best friend. I was happy and relieved and, for some weird reason, it all came out as tears.

When things calmed down a bit, Mrs. Shanahan gave us each an ice cream cone. We took them out to the front steps and tried to eat them faster than they were melting.

"I'm so excited that we're going to Florida," said Laini.

"I'm so excited that you're not *moving* to Florida," I said.

"Why didn't you tell me you thought I was moving?"

"Because if you would have been sad about moving to Florida, I figured it would be better if you didn't know until the last minute. Unless, of course, you would have been happy about moving to Florida."

"Without you? No way."

It felt good to have a friend who would choose me over Florida.

"Even though your grandma Shanahan is moving to Florida?" I asked.

"She's going to live in Florida for six months of the year and up here for the other six. So, same-same either way."

"You know, the reason I wanted a pet so bad," I confessed to Laini, "is that I thought maybe if I had a pet, I wouldn't be so lonely when you left."

"But you're still trying to get one, right? Because I really want you to still get one."

"I almost forgot to tell you! My parents said I

could get a pet because of reading the poem and buying the books for Reina. And Mr. Fermino said the animal shelter has way too many cats and kittens right now and all they're looking for is a small donation. Maybe my parents will pay it. If not, I would do backyard doggie poop cleanup for a whole week to earn it."

"I would help you," said Laini.

Only a true friend offers to help with backyard doggie poop cleanup.

"When do we get to go to the shelter?" asked Laini. Then she said, "Hey, I can be the pet's godmother! That is, if you would choose me to be its godmother."

"Nobody else but you," I answered. I was so happy, I didn't even care that my ice cream was melting all over my lucky shirt.

# SIXTEEN
# Charley

I tried my very best to walk calmly into the animal shelter. I figured that would be better than running in full speed and bursting through the door. They might not be so willing to give a pet to someone who looked like they had absolutely no self-control.

Laini was just as excited as I was. She squeezed my arm and said, "Remember the picture of the three kittens that Serenity found on the shelter's website? I wonder if they're still here."

"If I got all three, that would almost make up for not getting a baby pygmy goat," I said.

"Three?" Dad's voice pretty much told me my chances of leaving with three kittens were slim.

Amanda, the animal shelter volunteer, talked with us for a while and asked us some questions. Then she brought us into a room full of kittens who were running, jumping, and rolling over one another.

"I love this place!" said Laini.

"Look around, but it's best to let them come to you," Amanda said.

Laini sat on the floor, and the kittens had no problem coming over to her. A few climbed on her, and even though Laini's not the giggling type, she couldn't help but giggle when one licked her chin.

Across the hall, there were some cages with only one cat in each. I asked Amanda why they were by themselves.

"When they first come in, we keep them by themselves while we make sure they're not sick," Amanda said. "We don't want them to get any of the other cats sick."

I wandered over to the cages. One of the cats sat up with his head held up high. Even though it was a shelter cat in a cage, it still managed to look dignified. The tag on his cage said CHARLEY. TWO YEARS OLD. TABBY.

"What's he in for?" I asked Amanda.

"His owners had to move out of state and couldn't take him with them," she answered. "It's time for him to come out of quarantine. Would you like to see him?"

"Sure," I said. The kittens were cute but there was something about this cat named Charley.

"Fair warning, he tends to ignore most people," said Amanda as she opened Charley's cage. "Why don't you sit on the floor and give him a few minutes?"

I sat on the floor and waited while she set Charley down. He sat and just looked at me, still looking very dignified. I couldn't help but picture him with a crown on his head.

*Charley the feline king,* I thought.

"Hello, Charley," I said. Then I sat still and waited.

Charley got up and walked closer to me. I held out my hand, palm down, but didn't touch him. He sniffed my hand and then stretched and lay down next to me.

"It's good to meet you, Charley," I said, still not moving.

Charley looked up and then put his head on my lap. I reached my hand out slowly and scratched him behind the ears. He started to purr.

Laini came over and sat next to me. "This one likes you."

I nodded. "I think we just adopted each other."

"Are you okay with getting an ordinary pet instead of a baby pygmy goat? Or a kinkajou? Or a two-toed sloth?" asked Laini.

"I wanted an extraordinary pet to help replace an extraordinary friend," I told Laini. "But you're not leaving and, anyway, you're irreplaceable." I looked over at Charley. "Plus, I think Charley would be insulted if we called him ordinary."

"I thought you were going to name it Frederica. Or should we call him Fred?"

"No," I said. "He's Charley."

"But you said you wanted to give away your name."

"You can still call me Rica, but I think I'm going to keep my full name," I said. "Besides, he's a Charley. Definitely a Charley."

# SEVENTEEN
## Thank You

I didn't get a llama or an iguana or a baby pygmy goat, but I had a cat named Charley curled up next to me. And my very best friend, who *wasn't* moving, was sleeping over so she could help me take care of him.

I took out my prayer journal and wrote the shortest prayer I'd ever written:

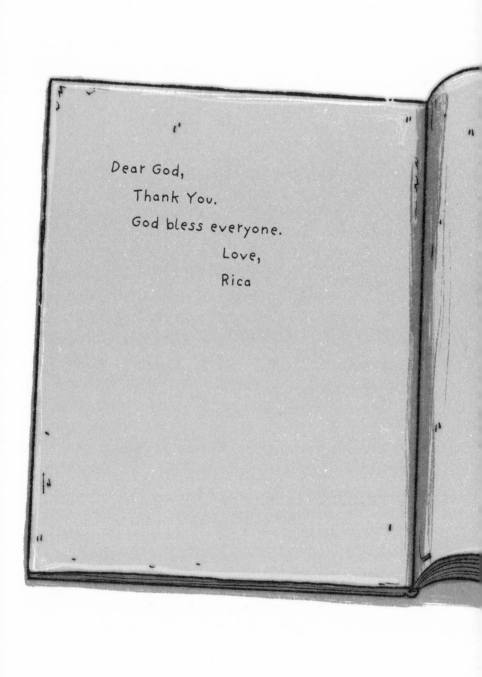

Dear God,
Thank You.
God bless everyone.
Love,
Rica